HEY DUGGEE

CHEER UP, PUP!

MEET DUGGEE.

He is a great big cuddly dog. Duggee is in charge
of all the fun and adventures at the clubhouse.

Would you like to meet Duggee's Squirrel Club?

NORRIE
is a kind
mouse.

BETTY
is a clever
octopus.

TAG
is a gentle
rhino.

ROLY
is a noisy
little hippo.

HAPPY
is a very happy
crocodile!

There is always something to do at Duggee's Clubhouse.
What will it be this time?

Someone's come to join in the fun today. Who is it?
It's Duggly, Duggee's little nephew.

"Hello, Duggly!" say the Squirrels. They love puppies.

"DU DU, DU DU!"
says Duggly. That means "Hello, Squirrels!" in puppy talk.

Duggly's on the move. What has he seen?

He wants to play with
Roly's truck.

But Duggly is a bit rough
with Roly's truck.

Roly isn't happy.

Now Duggly wants to play with Happy's spaceship.

Happy isn't happy any more.

Duggly has spotted Enid the cat having a lovely snooze.

But Duggly has not learned about being gentle.

DOINK!

Enid is REALLY not happy.
"Oh no! Poor Enid!" say the Squirrels.

The Squirrels need to find Duggly
something else to play with.
"Like what?" asks Norrie.

MEEEEEEEEOOOOOOOOWWWWWW!

"A puzzle?" suggests Happy.

No, that's too
difficult for Duggly.

"A jack-in-the-box?"
suggests Tag.

No, that's too scary
for Duggly.

"A rattle?" suggests Betty.

Yes, that's just perfect for Duggly!

RATTLE, RATTLE, RATTLE . . . OH!

"Why has he stopped?" asks Tag.
"Maybe he's broken," says Happy.

Oh dear!
"DUGGLY'S MADE A SMELL!"

"Make it stop, Duggee!" pleads Happy. "Woof woof!" woofs Duggee, pointing to his badge.

Duggee knows what to do.
He has his **PUPPY BADGE.**

Duggee gets to
work, and soon . . .

. . . Duggly is all clean again.
He smells much better now. **PHEW!**

Time for some fresh air!

"This is outside, Duggly," says Norrie. "Do you like it?"
Duggly giggles. He likes it.

"That's the sky," says Tag. "It's blue."

"That's a tree," says Betty. "It's green."

"That's Enid," says Roly, pointing to Enid.

"She's orange. And sleeping."

Duggly wants to play with Enid again, but Enid doesn't want to play with Duggly.

Oops. "Are you OK, Duggly?" asks Norrie.

Duggly is not OK. He starts crying.

"What do we do now?" the Squirrels ask.

"I know!" says Norrie. "Look, Duggly!" She blows a funny raspberry.

Has Duggly stopped crying?

No, Duggly has not stopped crying. Try again, Squirrels.

"Look, Duggly!" says Roly, making a funny noise.

"BWUUP!"

"Look, Duggly!" says Happy, making a funny face.

Has Duggly stopped crying? **NO!**

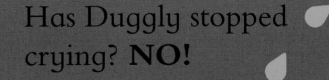

"Look, Duggly!" says Betty, blowing bubbles.

"Look, Duggly!" says Tag, jumping up and down.

Has Duggly stopped crying? **NO!**

Whatever the Squirrels try …

...Duggly won't stop crying! Until...

Has Duggly stopped crying? **YES!**
"Duggly loves Frog," says Happy. "Well done, Frog!"

Duggly shuts his eyes.
"He's asleep," whispers Norrie.
Ahh!

RIBBIT!

Haven't the Squirrels done well today, looking after Duggly? They've earned their . . .

PUPPY BADGE!

"Yay!" whisper the Squirrels, as quietly as they can. They don't want to wake Duggly! Just time for one more thing . . .

Can you earn your Puppy Badge? Do these activities, then write your name on the next page and ask an adult to help you cut it out.

Can you pull some funny faces, like the Squirrels did?

Pretend to be asleep. Do a GREAT BIG SNORE!

Have you got a toy you can look after today? Does it need a nappy change?

A baby dog is a puppy. Do you know what a baby cat is called? How about a baby pig?

Make up a little song to help someone go to sleep.

earned their
PUPPY BADGE